The Kiss of the Green Fairy

by

Jurgen Kleist

Contact: jurgenkleist.com

FADE IN:

SCREEN

Strands of white smoke are slowly rising upwards. A softly emerging breathing-in and breathing-out sound. Faint Music (à la Peter Gabriel's LONG WALK HOME.) The breathing sound and music mix to a climax...

DISSOLVE TO:

EXT. LONDON'S LIMEHOUSE DISTRICT -- DAY (1849)

ROBERT BUFORD, 25, handsome, well-dressed, belonging to the upper-class in Victorian England, walks down a deserted street in London's Limehouse district.

EXT./INT. OPIUM DEN/ROOM -- DAY

He enters an Opium Den and is greeted by a CHINESE MAN. Buford is led to a room at the back of the house. He pays the CHINESE MAN and sits down on the bed.

CHINESE
All day and all night?

BUFORD
All day and all night.

CHINESE
Good smoke arrived.

BUFORD
Must chase the demons away.

CHINESE
(not understanding)
No demons in the house.

BUFORD
(smiling)
I mean the demons in my head. Bring some Absinthe, too.

The CHINESE MAN nods and disappears. BUFORD makes himself comfortable and reclines on the bed. After a short while the CHINESE appears with a tablet on which there is a bottle of Absinthe, sugar cubes, water for the preparation of the drink, and an opium pipe, an oil lamp and opium. He puts it carefully on the table besides the bed and begins the preparation of the Absinthe.

(CONTINUED)

CONTINUED:

He pours a glass half-full with Absinthe, then places a special spoon over the glass, on which he places a sugar cube. Then he pours water over the sugar which melts. He then prepares the opium pipe and places it next to the Absinthe glass. He then bows and disappears. Buford takes a sip from the Absinthe glass and then lights the pipe. He inhales deeply. He drinks again, refills the glass, and takes another smoke. He finishes the glass, and smokes again, then he reclines on the bed, pulls the blanket over his body and closes his eyes...

The den door opens and the GREEN FAIRY appears. The Green Fairy is a tall, thin (Cate Blanchett-like) woman with a flowing dress that reveals her figure. She has long, black hair. The Green Fairy glides through the room and sits down on Buford's bed. She gives him a kiss on the forehead...

THE DREAM:

EXT. OXFORD (ENGLAND) -- DAY (1849)

A Chapel, surrounded by greenery. Out of the Chapel comes Music: Vivaldi's "Stabat Mater."

INT. CHAPEL -- DAY

A communion. Circa TWENTY YOUNG MEN are kneeling down and receive their blessings. The altar is illuminated by candle light. Music is playing. The PRIEST readies for the prayer.

PRIEST
Now, let us pray together: Pater noster, qui es in caelis: sanctificetur nomen tuum; adveniat regnum tuum; fiat voluntas Tua, sicut in caelo, et in terra. Panem nostrum cotidianum da nobis hodie; et dimitte nobis debita nostra, sicut et nos dimittimus debitoribus nostris; et ne nos inducas in tentationem; sed libera nos a malo...

While the PRIEST'S voice fades off, JONATHAN WHITE, 25, handsome, is looking to the VIRGIN MARY above the altar. His hands are folded in prayer, his eyes are wide-open. JONATHAN, together with the other YOUNG PRIESTS.

JONATHAN
Amen.

(CONTINUED)

CONTINUED:

PRIEST
Please rise!

The YOUNG PRIESTS rise quietly.

PRIEST
Once upon a time there was a young man... He was the pride of his parents, who worked hard on their land, harvesting the goods that God had provided them with.
(beat)
Tall and handsome, he was, our young man, oh yes, and the fair maidens had laid their lovely eyes upon him. But he walked by them, without paying attention because he saw something that no maiden could give him: the destiny of his life. Our beloved Mother Mary stood there, silently, yet overflowing with wisdom, and she reached out and embraced our young man with that love, only the church can give. Our young man found his happiness in the arms of the church, and he's never let go of that image because it was burned into his soul at that very moment. Since then, he longed for the embrace of a virgin ... Mary... our... Mother ... the church.

While the PRIEST says "a virgin", some YOUNG PRIESTS look at each other... The priest, moved by his own words, clears his throat. He continues in a sinister tone.

PRIEST
Today is the most important day of your lives. As God's new missionaries, you represent the Church as well as the high ideals England stands for. We have given the world freedom, civility, and prosperity. Britain's might and pride reaches from shore to shore, from continent to continent. Britain not only rules the seas, it rules the souls as well ... for there is only one God ... there is only one Queen...there is only one England! It is your mission to take God's word to the farthest lands and to the farthest shores.
(MORE)

(CONTINUED

CONTINUED:

PRIEST (cont'd)
You will be the ambassadors of freedom and justice, equality and brotherhood. God bless you. Long live the Crown, long live England.

The YOUNG PRIESTS, one by one, approach the PRIEST, and kiss his hand.

INT. WHITE'S HOME -- EVENING

The FAMILY is sitting around the dinner table. They eat in silence. From time to time, Jonathan's MOTHER dries her eyes. His FATHER stares at the dinner plate. Jonathan's younger brother PETER, 17, plays with his fork and looks intently at Jonathan, and his younger sister MARY, 15, looks at her mother.

FATHER
I suppose you've packed?

JONATHAN
Of course, father.

MOTHER
And you promise you'll write as soon as you arrive?

JONATHAN
Of course, mother. As soon as I'm on board I'll write to you. I'll write down everything I see and hear. And once I am in Panama, I'll send you a letter every day.

FATHER
(smiling)
Well, young man, every day might be a bit much. They won't have that much ink in Panama.

Everyone laughs.

JONATHAN
(excited)
Every week at least. At least.
(he sighs)
Oh mother, don't be sad. Think of me not as your lost son, think of me as an ambassador, as ... God's ambassador. Where I am, England is ... and where England is, there is the Lord.

(CONTINUED)

CONTINUED:

PETER
Will you become a Saint when you come back?

JONATHAN
(laughing)
No, Peter, I don't think so. To become a Saint, you have to do more than what I do, you have to be more than human.

FATHER
It is time to finish our supper. Tomorrow is another day, and for Jonathan a new life begins.

MARY
Will you send me a present? A monkey doll?

MOTHER
Be quiet, Mary. Don't ask silly questions. We don't even know whether those people have dolls like we do.

MARY
But if they have dolls, can Jonathan send me one?

FATHER
I'm sure he will. But it's late, and we should go to bed now.
(beat)
Jonathan. We are very proud of you. And we know that you will do your best to ...

MOTHER
(crying)
Please, please...

FATHER
(clearing his throat)
Well, I'm not a man of words. God bless you, son. Here,
(he reaches into his pocket)
a present from your mother and me.

Jonathan receives a necklace with a cross. He looks at it, then he kisses it, and puts it around his neck.

(CONTINUED)

CONTINUED:

JONATHAN
Thank you Father. Thank you Mother. You will be proud of me. God bless you all.

EXT. SOUTHAMPTON HARBOR -- EVENING

JONATHAN walks down a seedy street which is full of SAILORS, STREET PEDDLERS, PROSTITUTES. He looks around with wonderment. A DRUNKEN SAILOR collapses at a street corner. Jonathan walks to a seedy hotel. He passes a line of young PROSTITUTES. The girls are dressed provocatively, their hairs are teased up, their lips bright red. While he is passing by, they advertise themselves.

FIRST WHORE
Hey, handsome. Want some ripe peaches?

SECOND WHORE
If you're looking for a juicy plum, don't go any further.

THIRD WHORE
Hey angel, let me take you under my wings.

JONATHAN looks away and speeds up his steps. He finds a hotel that features the sign "Rooms." He checks in.

INT. RECEPTION -- HOTEL

RECEPTIONIST, older, ragged, is sitting at the desk.

RECEPTIONIST
And that would be for how many nights?

JONATHAN
One, only one.

RECEPTIONIST
Moving on?

JONATHAN
Tomorrow morning.

RECEPTIONIST
To the Americas?

CONTINUED:

JONATHAN
Yes. But how do you know?

RECEPTIONIST
(laughing)
The first ship in the morning is the one that sails to the Americas. It's called "Fortune 2."

JONATHAN
That's the one.

RECEPTIONIST
(mumbling)
I always wonder what's happened to "Fortune 1."

He shows JONATHAN his room, has him pay for it, then leaves him standing there. Jonathan looks at the bed. He puts his bag on a chair, opens it, gets out his priest outfit, dresses, and goes down the stairs to the RECEPTIONIST.

JONATHAN
Would you know of a decent eatery around here?

He looks astonished at JONATHAN in his priest outfit.

RECEPTIONIST
Holy Father... Decent eatery?

JONATHAN
Anything, really. I haven't eaten since this morning.

RECEPTIONIST
Down the road. Father. The one with no sign. They broke it off, those drunken bastard... forgive me my language.

JONATHAN
(ignoring it)
Far?

RECEPTIONIST
Few steps.

JONATHAN nods a "thank you", then walks out of the hotel.

EXT. SOUTHAMPTON STREET -- NIGHT

The street is busier than before. Hordes of SAILORS, arm in arm, walk down the street. Somewhere at a corner there is a fight. One hears yelling, cursing and shouting. A SAILOR walks by with TWO WHORES in his arms. Some well-dressed GENTLEMEN,too, pass by. A BEGGAR sits at an entrance and shows his missing leg. The smell, the noise, the whirl of people seems too much for JONATHAN who is both fascinated and repulsed by this sight. He stops at a lamp post and leans against it. A LITTLE BOY sneaks up on him.

LITTLE BOY
Have you got any money, mister... sir...
(recognizing Jonathan's priest outfit)
... Father?

JONATHAN
(absent-minded)
What... do you want...?

LITTLE BOY
(bowing, grabbing Jonathan's hand)
Money. Me mother is sick. I need to...

JONATHAN reaches into his pocket and fishes out a few coins. He gives them to the BOY.

JONATHAN
God bless you, my boy.

The BOY bites on one of the coins. Then he nods.

LITTLE BOY
Thanks, Father.

JONATHAN walks on, finds the restaurant with the absent sign, and enters.

INT. RESTAURANT -- NIGHT

Thick smoke waves through the room. The tables are filled with MEN, drinking, gambling, talking. In a corner he sees some well-dressed GENTLEMEN with young WHORES on their knees. JONATHAN orders a soup, bread, and water. While he eats silently, he observes his surroundings.

(CONTINUED)

CONTINUED:

A "FLOWER GIRL" (16), slender, pretty, with a bucket of flowers comes to his table. She looks at him, scanning his face to see whether he understands this kind of soliciting business.

FLOWER GIRL
Please, would you like to buy some, sir? My rose is fresh.

JONATHAN, (not getting this soliciting act by a prostitute), buys a rose. Suddenly the FLOWER GIRL begins to sob (to keep his attention). Jonathan tries to calm her. An OLDER WOMAN (part of the act) comes by and takes the girl by her hand.

OLDER WOMAN
Sorry, Father. But her mother died a week ago. The girl is still up-set. Sorry. Let's go, girl. Be quiet.

JONATHAN swirls the rose in his hand until the head breaks off. He is up-set. He eats his meal.

MEANWHILE:

EXT. SOUTHAMPTON -- HARBOR QUARTER -- NIGHT

A well-dressed ROBERT BUFORD crosses the street and enters a bar.

INT. BAR -- NIGHT

The bar is filled with MEN who drink and gamble. BUFORD is walking towards a table where THREE WELL-DRESSED MEN are sitting. They are waiting for his arrival. Buford fetches a chair and sits down. He is pulling out of his jacket a stack of DOCUMENTS and lays them on the table. Each document bears an official-looking stamp and the printed name: "Sutter's Mill. Gold Certificate".

BUFORD
Here it is, Gentlemen. Fifteen Gold Certificates, which arrived this morning from San Francisco, California, and ready to be sold.

He leans back and lights a cigar. Each of the GENTLEMAN takes a Gold Certificate and examines it.

(CONTINUED)

CONTINUED:

BUFORD
Ready to be sold, gentlemen. Each Certificate is worth 1/2 an acre of land under which there is gold.

BUFORD pulls out of his jacket a small leather bag and opens it. He pours its content on the table. Small gold nuggets fall onto it. The Gentlemen sigh at the sight of it. One takes a nugget up and examines it closely.

FIRST GENTLEMAN
How much do you want for the Certificates?

BUFORD collects the gold nuggets and puts them back into the bag.

BUFORD
Each is worth 100 pounds but I give them to you for 75. You easily fetch 150 or more for one.

SECOND GENTLEMAN
That is too good to be true...

BUFORD
Yes, it is. Because there is more to come. I bought one hundred more Certificates, they'll arrive in a month.

THIRD GENTLEMAN
I am in.

He takes four Certificates and pulls out money, which he lays on the table. The other GENTLEMEN do the same. BUFORD collects the money and puts it into his jacket pocket.

BUFORD
Gentlemen. I'll meet you a month from now.

He gets up and walks out of the bar. The Gentlemen nod a greeting and wait until BUFORD has disappeared.

FIRST GENTLEMAN
I think we've got him.

SECOND GENTLEMAN
Inspector Murray and his men will apprehend him as we speak. Buford usually goes to the brothel when he made a deal.

(CONTINUED)

CONTINUED:

THIRD GENTLEMAN
Very well, I think it is time to have a drink.

EXT. SOUTHAMPTON STREET -- NIGHT

BUFORD is walking towards a brothel at the end of the street. When he is about to enter the building, he finds himself surrounded by THREE POLICEMEN who apprehend him. But Buford manages to slip away and runs into the brothel. The policemen curse and follow him inside.

INT. FOYER -- NIGHT

The foyer of the brothel is filled with well-dressed, upper-class MEN and PROSTITUTES who are lounging on sofas and chairs, smoking, drinking. BUFORD runs up the stairs and disappears in one of the rooms. The entrance of the POLICEMEN causes considerable chaos among the prostitutes and especially among the men. Some hide their faces, some run into rooms; the prostitutes protest and yell obscenities. The policemen look around, then one is running up the stairs, opening door after door in which...

INT. SEVERAL ROOMS

PROSTITUTES and CLIENTS are involved in various acts of love making.

INT. ROOM

Meanwhile BUFORD climbs through the window and jumps into an adjacent garden.

EXT. GARDEN -- NIGHT

He gets up, touches his jacket to see whether the money is in it but realizes to his horror that he has lost it...

BUFORD
God damn! What now?

BACK TO:

INT. RESTAURANT -- NIGHT

JONATHAN pays for his meal and steps outside the restaurant.

EXT. SOUTHAMPTON -- STREET -- NIGHT

Across the street, the OLDER WOMAN whispers something into the ears of the "FLOWER GIRL" who nods and walks swiftly after Jonathan. She catches up with him, passes by and then runs into him, trips and falls in front of Jonathan. He almost stumbles over her. The "Flower Girl" starts sobbing. Jonathan recognizes her and he bends down.

JONATHAN
I'm so sorry, so sorry. How did that happen?

He shakes his head in disbelieve.

JONATHAN
Come, here.

He gives her his hand and pulls her up.

FLOWER GIRL
(wiping her tears)
It was my fault, sir...Father.

She tries to wipe off some dust from JONATHAN'S frock.

JONATHAN
(looking around)
Where is that lady you were with some moments ago?

FLOWER GIRL
(crying again)
She is a bad lady.

JONATHAN
What do you mean? I don't understand!

FLOWER GIRL
She stole all my flowers and my money.

JONATHAN
(confused)
So she was not with you? But in the restaurant, you were together...!

FLOWER GIRL
No, she is a stranger. I don't know that woman.
(MORE)

(CONTINUED)

CONTINUED:

FLOWER GIRL (cont'd)
(beat, crying again)
Now she is off with all my money and the roses. What am I supposed to do? It's late...I have no place to stay.

JONATHAN
(hesitating)
I can give you some money.

FLOWER GIRL
Money? Here? They rob me right away. Just look around. Do you see that they eye us already?

JONATHAN is looking around, and indeed, several shady CHARACTERS look at him and the girl. Especially the CON ARTIST ROBERT BUFORD has his eyes set on both. He stands in a doorway and studies Jonathan and the FLOWER GIRL closely.

FLOWER GIRL (cont'd)
(grabbing his hand)
Where could I go now? I am all alone. Please help me, Father!

JONATHAN
(firm)
Come.

He grabs the GIRL by the hand, and they walk off. Keeping a distance, BUFORD is following them.

JONATHAN (cont'd)
You can stay with me tonight. I have a room. But I'll leave tomorrow. I am Father Jonathan White. And what's your name?

FLOWER GIRL
They call me Dolly. . . Nice to meet you, Father.

INT. HOTEL LOBBY -- NIGHT

The RECEPTIONIST is sitting at the desk. JONATHAN and the FLOWER GIRL walk in. He still is holding her by the hand. Jonathan sees the Receptionist and suddenly realizes how this must appear to the Receptionist. But the Receptionist just grins at the two and nods his head, seemingly understanding. He wants to say something, but the Girl, unnoticed by Jonathan, puts her finger over her lips and silences the Receptionist.

CONTINUED:

JONATHAN
(hasty)
This girl needs help. She is all alone, besides her mother died, and someone stole her money and her roses.

RECEPTIONIST
Yes, of course, Father. Very understandable, and very laudable too. Poor girl. She is lucky, she's found a helping hand.

JONATHAN
Well, it's my duty.

RECEPTIONIST
Of course, it is, Father. Of course it is.

JONATHAN
Well, then. Good night.

He grabs the FLOWER GIRL by the hand and walks off with her to his room.

INT. HOTEL ROOM -- NIGHT

Both enter the room.

JONATHAN
(firm)
Now, you clean yourself up and then you sleep over there on that bed.

He points to a second bed in the corner.

FLOWER GIRL
Yes, Father.

JONATHAN
What's your real name, little girl?

FLOWER GIRL
Marie, Father.

JONATHAN
You seem to have a French accent...

But before he gets an answer, the GIRL disappears in the bathroom. Meanwhile, JONATHAN kneels in front of his bed, praying silently.

CONTINUED:

When the GIRL reappears, washed, her hair flowing, her dress a bit different, Jonathan is still praying with his eyes closed. The girl walks to the bed and lies down. She pulls the blanket over her body. Jonathan finishes his prayer, opens his eyes and gets up. He looks at the girl. Then he goes into the bathroom and closes the door. While he is in the bathroom, the girl takes off her clothes, but then she pulls the blanket up to her chin again. When Jonathan returns, he looks at the girl again, who has by now closed her eyes, then he lies down in the other bed and blows out the candle. Then he undresses himself, puts the cross on the night stand, slips under the sheet, folds his hands, and closes his eyes. He drifts into sleep. During the night, Jonathan has a DREAM.

JONATHAN'S DREAM:

INT. CHAPEL -- OXFORD -- DAY

The Chapel is decorated with candles and flowers. JONATHAN is walking down the aisle. At his side is the FLOWER GIRL who is dressed in a bride's outfit and looks beautiful. Her long hair is flowing. Both smile at each other. Jonathan greets his PARENTS, his SIBLINGS and FELLOW YOUNG PRIESTS from the seminary. But the PRIEST who ordained him looks scornfully at Jonathan and his bride. The priest lifts his finger scolding both, but Jonathan only smiles at the priest and walks by. Jonathan and his Bride come to a halt in front of the altar. He looks up to the STATUE of the MOTHER MARY-- but instead of her he sees now a black void in the form of the statue. In slow motion, heads of roses begin to fall out of this statue. Images of DRUNKEN MEN, half-naked WHORES, a ship, Indian faces, a YOUNG BOY biting on a coin, peaches, plums, naked breasts ... These images increase in speed until a whirlwind of images flickers across the screen. Then the following image emerges:

INT. HOTEL ROOM -- NIGHT

JONATHAN is lying naked in his bed and the FLOWER GIRL, also naked, is on top of him, making love to him ... Rose pedals are floating down on them.

JONATHAN
(whispering,
passionate)
I love you. I love you.

The FLOWER GIRL is bending down and is caressing his chest with her hair. The image is fading away...

CONTINUED:

DISSOLVE TO:

INT. HOTEL ROOM -- NEXT MORNING

JONATHAN opens his eyes and yawns. Morning light falls through the window. He looks to his left, and to his surprise, the FLOWER GIRL is sleeping next to him. He jumps up, looking around, to the couch, then back to the Flower Girl next to him. She looks beautiful, has soft features, her hair falls over the sheet. Jonathan, still confused, grabs the cross from the night stand and holds it to his heart. He closes his eyes and his lips move silently in prayer. But once in a while he opens them to see whether the girl is still lying there---as if it were a dream. He then gets up slowly, making no noise. He gets into his priest outfit, picks up his bag, and tip-toes to the door. There he turns around and looks again at the sleeping girl. He hesitates for a moment, then he puts his bag down, pulls out money from his pocket, tip-toes back, and puts it on the night stand. He takes a last look at the sleeping girl, with sadness in his eyes. Swiftly, he turns around and closes the door. Then, there is a commotion outside the door.

BUFORD (O.S.)
What in the hell did you do to that little girl, bloody bastard? Eh? Knocking her good?

JONATHAN (O.S.)
I... I don't know what you mean... Who are you?

BUFORD (O.S.)
Pedophile priest.

Hard blows follow, and a BODY falls down the stairs. Then, suddenly, all is quiet.

INT. HOTEL ROOM -- MORNING

BUFORD enters the room where the GIRL still is. He walks toward the bed. The girl looks at him... Then, Buford tears away the blanket she is holding in front of her. The girl's breasts are visible...

FLOWER GIRL (O.S.)
Please, don't... no...no...

EXT. SOUTHAMPTON -- STREET

We see from a distance the CON MAN ROBERT BUFORD, dressed in JONATHAN'S priest outfit, leaving the hotel. He is walking to the harbor, boarding the ship "Fortune 2" which will take him to Panama. From now on, he assumes WHITE'S identity.

CUT TO:

EXT. PANAMA CITY -- DAY (1849)

A seedy quarter, a dirty street, a cheap hotel. Ragged people run around.

INT. SEEDY HOTEL ROOM -- DAY

The curtains are closed, and the room is lit by candles. BUFORD, his face is swollen and bandaged, is lying on a bed. His head is propped up by pillows. A bible is lying on a night stand next to him. Also next to him, sitting on his bedside, is the prostitute MARIE, 16, slender, pretty. A scar marks her face. She is the "FLOWER GIRL" from Southampton, but Buford does not recognize her! Marie is preparing an opium pipe. She lights it, then passes the pipe to BUFORD, who takes it, nods thankfully to Marie, and then inhales deeply. He keeps the smoke long in his lungs, then exhales slowly. He gives the pipe back to Marie, who puts the pipe aside, and sinks back into the pillows. Buford closes his eyes for a moment, smiles, and then opens them again. He looks at the girl and touches her small breasts. Marie moves back a bit, then she is taking Buford's hand, kissing his fingers for a brief moment, putting them on her lap.

MARIE
Voulez-vous un dejeuneur?

BUFORD
Speak English with me, Marie.

MARIE
Lunch? Je fame. I'm really hungry. I get us some fruit and bread? D'accord?

BUFORD
I'm not hungry.

He fetches the pipe, lights it and inhales.

(CONTINUED)

CONTINUED:

BUFORD

Besides,

(he exhales)

if I let you go, you might not return.

MARIE

As long as you pay me, I'll stay with you. So you don't have to worry.

BUFORD

Lie down. I want to touch your skin.

MARIE

Je fame... I'm hungry...I haven't eaten since last night's morning.

BUFORD

(smiling faintly)

...last night's morning... it's yesterday morning. In English we say since yesterday mor...

MARIE

(interrupting)

...what does it matter! Je fame. I'm bloody hungry.

(with drama)

I'll faint, if I don't get anything now.

BUFORD

(grabbing her hand)

Promise me, Marie, that you'll come back.

MARIE gets up, withdrawing her hand from BUFORD'S rather forcefully. Then stretching her hand out to him again. She looks coldly at Buford.

MARIE

I need money.

He's rolling slightly over to the side and he points to the mattress.

BUFORD

There.

MARIE is sliding her hand under the mattress and fetching a couple of bills. She counts them.

(CONTINUED)

CONTINUED:

MARIE
Anything else, monsieur?

BUFORD is fetching the pipe and lifting it up.

BUFORD
More of this!

MARIE is putting the money into her purse, dresses and leaves the room. BUFORD takes another draw from the pipe and sinks back into the pillows. He closes his eyes.

FLASH BACK:

EXT. SEEDY STREET -- PANAMA CITY -- PREVIOUS NIGHT

A seedy, noisy street in Panama City which is called "Sin Alley." There are bars, a brothel, and drunken SAILORS, swaggering about; in the distance, there is a fight... A DRUNKEN SAILOR (tall, strong, 20) is walking by the brothel. BUFORD, in his priest garb, is passing by. He is clutching to his chest a big Bible. THREE PROSTITUTES (one of them is MARIE) are standing in front of the entrance and are chatting with each other, oblivious of the approaching sailor. Marie, however, watches closely Buford who is approaching the group. She signals the DRUNKEN SAILOR who is also watching Buford coming closer. The sailor staggers by, then stops, looks at the PROSTITUTES, and grabs MARIE. The prostitutes protest loudly which attracts Buford's attention. He stands and watches, as the drunken sailor drags Marie to a nearby alley and begins to rip her clothes off. Buford hears Marie screaming. Buford walks towards the alley, sees the sailor and Marie in a fight, then he walks up to the two, and hits the sailor with the Bible on his head. The sailor lets up, turns around and throws a couple of hard blows at Buford who goes down immediately. Then the sailor spits at Buford and walks away. Buford holds his chin and moans. Marie bends down and comforts him. Buford's face is bloody.

MARIE
Sorry. So sorry!

BUFORD
I need help.

MARIE
Let's go to a place I know.

She helps BUFORD to get up, and they both walk down the street to a hotel. MARIE takes care of the formalities with the CONCIERGE, and they both walk to a room.

CONTINUED:

She helps Buford to lie down on a bed. Buford is in pain, he holds his chin.

BACK TO:

INT. SEEDY HOTEL ROOM -- PANAMA CITY -- DAY

MARIE returns with a bag full of groceries. She puts it on the table. She wipes her forehead.

MARIE
Oh, la la, Hot, very hot. Voila, monsieur. Fruit, pain blanc, jabon, miel, cafe..et un journal "Panama Times."

BUFORD is opening his swollen eyes, watching MARIE.

BUFORD
Did you also get some opium?

MARIE
I'll make us lunch, d'accord?

BUFORD
I'm not hungry.

MARIE
But, monsieur...Jonathan...you must eat! When was the last time you eat?

BUFORD
...You ate. In English it is "ate".

MARIE
Tres bien... when did you ate last?

BUFORD
It's "eat"..when did you eat, not ate..."

MARIE
You speak a strange language. One can only guess. So, when have you...had some food?

BUFORD
Yesterday, last week...I don't remember.

MARIE
It wasn't last week.

(CONTINUED)

CONTINUED:

BUFORD
How do you know?

MARIE steps to BUFORD'S bed, bending down.

MARIE
Because, we only met last night.

BUFORD
Only last night? It feels as if I have known you for...a week, or maybe two.

MARIE is pointing to the pipe.

MARIE
You smoke too much! Opium makes you believe that one hour lasts an eternity. That's why I hardly ever smoke when I am with a customer.

BUFORD
Why?

MARIE
Do I really want to make it seem like an eternity when a fat, drunken man is lying on me? Besides, nobody pays for eternity.

MARIE walks to the table and begins to eat some fruit. Then she makes a sandwich. She looks at BUFORD who wants to fill the pipe again. Marie gets up and walks back to the bed. She gives Buford the sandwich.

MARIE (cont'd)
Here. Eat.

BUFORD is grabbing her hand with the sandwich.

BUFORD
Why do you want me to eat?

MARIE
Because if you don't eat, you'll die; and if you're dead, I don't get paid.

BUFORD
You are smart.

CONTINUED:

MARIE
No, I'm not. If I were smart, I would live in a nice place, have a husband and children, but I would not be living in this hell-hole, called Panama City.

BUFORD
So, why did you end up here?

MARIE
My story ... what do you care about a story from a French girl... you promised me to tell me your story. An young, handsome English priest, by the name of Jonathan White...here, in Panama City? Besides, you also promised me that if I listened to your story, you would double my fee.

BUFORD
Really? I don't remember that part.

MARIE
But I do! ... As I said earlier...you smoke too much.

BUFORD is reclining, lighting the pipe, having a puff.

BUFORD
Alright then...Everything has a purpose in life. Mine was... to come here.

BUFORD looks at MARIE who is finishing her lunch. She gets up and opens the curtains. Bright light falls into the room. She opens the window, street noise is audible.

BUFORD (cont'd)
Close the window, and draw the curtain close too. I hate bright light.

MARIE
Fresh air is good for you.

She closes the window and draws the curtain.

BUFORD
(mocking her a bit)
Food is good for you, fresh air is good ... you seem to know about the good things in life.

(CONTINUED)

CONTINUED:

MARIE
(shooting back)
And you about all the bad things in life.

BUFORD
I was so naive when I arrived. Young and naive. And so full of hope that I could change the world a bit, that I could make a difference in peoples' lives.

MARIE
Maybe you did. Maybe you changed someone's life...

BUFORD
Here? In this hell hole? When God created hell, he had Panama in mind.

MARIE
There are many forms of hell.

BUFORD is looking at MARIE. She looks at him in a cold way.

BUFORD
(irritated)
You are young. What do you know about hell?!

MARIE
A thing or two. But you wanted to tell me your story.

BUFORD
Ah, yes. My story. Where was I?

MARIE
You arrived in Panama, you said... young and naive.

BUFORD
Yes, and I should have known better...

DISSOLVE TO:

EXT. MISSIONARY'S HOUSE -- COLON -- DAY

BUFORD walks to the door, sets his bag down and knocks. A few moments later, the door is opened by a young INDIAN WOMAN who holds a shotgun in her hand. Buford steps back when he sees the shotgun.

BUFORD
Excuse me...Madam...my name is Father White, I am from England, I was told to see Father McKenzie...here...

He pulls out a letter and waves it at the INDIAN WOMAN. The woman looks back into the house. Suddenly, the voice of RONALD CHESTER is coming from inside.

CHESTER (O.S)
Who the hell is that?

INDIAN WOMAN
A man is here.

CHESTER (O.S)
I don't want to see nobody. Send him away!

INDIAN WOMAN
He is a priest.

CHESTER (O.S)
Especially then, send him away. Or better: shoot him!

INDIAN WOMAN
You heard him. Better leave.

BUFORD
(confused)
But I was told Father McKenzie would receive me and instruct me in my duties. Here
(he waves the letter again)
...here it states...

CHESTER (O.S)
(yelling)
Let him in!

INT. ROOM

The INDIAN WOMAN steps aside, and BUFORD walks in. The room is kept dark. RONALD CHESTER, 62, run-down, unshaven, is sitting on a rocking chair, a bottle of rum is standing next to him.

BUFORD
Father McKenzie?

He steps forward to shake CHESTER'S hand, but the man reaches for the bottle.

CHESTER
(taking a swig)
Save the niceties. What brings you here?

BUFORD
I was told...back in Oxford...to see you. You are heading this mission, and ... here, this is the letter with the instructions and your address.

BUFORD is handing CHESTER a letter.

CHESTER
(cutting in, ignoring the letter)
...Want a drink?

BUFORD
No thank you.

CHESTER
(drinks again)
I thought so.

The CHESTER looks intently at BUFORD who is still standing and getting uncomfortable.

CHESTER (cont'd)
Let me give you an advise. The advise of a man who has spent the last seven years here in Colon. Get out of here, and do it fast! This place is hell on earth, and if there is a God, it must be an evil God. Now, take my advice and leave me alone!

BUFORD
But Father McKenzie...

CONTINUED:

CHESTER
(yelling)
You have no idea what I have been through! Go back, young man, go back to England!
(now soft)
And do yourself the favor and kill that man who sent you here.
(now yelling)
Kill him! Kill him! Kill him... because it is the same one that sent me here...
(he suddenly starts sobbing)
...who sent me here, seven years ago...sent me to this place, to this Devil's paradise...yes, that's what it is: A Devil's paradise.

CHESTER is sobbing hard now. He throws the bottle on the floor. The INDIAN WOMAN escorts BUFORD to the door. Buford steps outside.

EXT. MISSIONARY'S HOUSE -- DAY

INDIAN WOMAN
(whispering)
Father McKenzie died last year. Mr. Chester,
(she points back to the house)
he was his right hand at church service. He found Father McKenzie one day in the jungle... Since then he wears the priest's dress once a week and walks through town, blessing all the people.

She puts her finger to her head, indicating that he is insane.

INDIAN WOMAN
I worry.

BUFORD is clearly irritated.

BUFORD
Father McKenzie, dead? How did he die?

INDIAN WOMAN, looking back into the house to make sure Mr. Chester doesn't hear her.

(CONTINUED)

CONTINUED:

INDIAN WOMAN
He was found naked... killed the Indian way.

BUFORD is curious now.

BUFORD
The Indian way? I don't understand.

INDIAN WOMAN
The Indians torture and kill people by slitting open their stomach.

BUFORD
And?

INDIAN WOMAN
And then they pull out a part of the intestines.

BUFORD
And then?

INDIAN WOMAN (O.S.)
And then they nail the intestines to the tree.... and then they ... they whip the person around the tree.

CUT TO:

EXT. JUNGLE -- DAY

A MAN is driven around a tree by INDIANS with whips. His intestines are wrapping around the tree. The Indians laugh and shout, birds cry, monkeys fly through the air...

CUT BACK TO:

EXT. MISSIONARY'S HOUSE -- DAY

MR. CHESTER is yelling from inside the house again, he is howling like a wolf.

INDIAN WOMAN
I must go now. He needs my help.

She closes the door. BUFORD picks up his bag and staggers away. Buford is walking with his bag through main street, downtown. The street is muddy, left and right, there are seedy bars, houses, shops...everything is falling apart and kept standing by meager means.

CONTINUED:

KIDS play naked in the mud, WOMEN are sitting on porches, nursing BABIES, OLD MEN rock in chairs and drink rum, YOUNG MEN stand together in gangs and eye passers by. Some throw knives into a wall. Buford walks by, dressed in his priest suit, a cross hanging around his neck. He neither looks right nor left. He walks as if he had a goal in mind, his eyes are fixed to a point in front of him. The people on the porches, the kids, they all look at him as he passes by. Buford reaches the end of the street, he looks at the wasteland before him, then he turns around and walks back with the same determination as before. One of the boys in the gang is throwing a knife at Buford which flies by his head by only a few inches. Buford hears laughter in the distance. But he doesn't look back and proceeds. In front of him, up the hill, is the house of "Father McKenzie" again. He walks up to it and puts his bag down in front of the door. He knocks. After a moment, the INDIAN WOMAN opens, she holds now a shotgun in her hand.

EXT. MISSIONARY'S HOUSE -- DAY

INDIAN WOMAN
What is it this time?

BUFORD
(desperate)
What am I supposed to do now?

The INDIAN WOMAN is looking into the interior.

INDIAN WOMAN
(whispering)
I don't know. Mr. Chester wouldn't want you here. Since Father McKenzie is dead, he has taken his place. Once a week, he now is going into town to bless the people. Besides, he also collects alms when he is out. Pays for his rum. Have you tried the railroad?

BUFORD
The railroad? What do you mean?

INDIAN WOMAN
They're building a railroad across the isthmus. Maybe you could speak with them.

BUFORD
Where is it?

(CONTINUED)

CONTINUED:

INDIAN WOMAN
Just a few miles down the road.

BUFORD
Down the road? There are no roads here. It is only mud and swamps.

INDIAN WOMAN
Well, then it is only a few miles down the swamps... Good luck!

EXT. MISSIONARY'S HOUSE -- DAY

She closes the door because one could hear MR. CHESTER moaning inside. BUFORD lifts up his bag and walks on.

EXT. STREET -- DAY

After a few moments Buford stops and puts down the bag beside him. He looks at his boots, which are covered in mud, mosquitoes are humming in force everywhere. Wiping the sweat off his forehead, he slowly scans his surroundings, squinting against the harsh sun. His eyes wander to a group of young BOYS who are nearby playing with a dog.

BUFORD
(shouting)
You ... boys! Know where the railroad office is?

The BOYS stop what they are doing, look at each other and start giggling.

BUFORD
Do you hear me? Comprende? Train? El tren? You know how to get there?

A SMALL BOY from the group starts running towards BUFORD.

SMALL BOY
Si, senor, si. I know where go. Come, come! Lots people! Big noise!

The small BOY gestures to BUFORD, his FRIENDS come running. The dog starts yelping and runs too.

BUFORD
So you know where to go? You really know, don't you. All right, you get me there and
(MORE)

(CONTINUED)

CONTINUED:

BUFORD (cont'd)
(pulling a few coins from his pocket)
these will be yours.

OTHER BOYS
(shrieking with delight and excitement)
Si, senor! You come with us, we show. No far, no far!

BUFORD
All right, then. Let's go.

EXT. A CONSTRUCTION SITE -- COLON -- DAY

BUFORD looks around. He is standing on a small hill. Several miles of tracks are already laid. They disappear into the jungle where one can see MEN standing up to their hips in the swamp, cursing, working, being yelled at by SUPERVISORS. Heavy machinery lifts tracks. Sand and debris is dumped into the swamp to build an underground. It is brutally hot, the air is humid, hazy, steaming. Swarms of mosquitoes move like clouds. The sound of the nearby jungle is clearly audible. Strange, colorful birds sit on branches and squawk; little monkeys move from tree to tree; gigantic ants, carrying big leafs, march along their trail. A WHITE FOREMAN, who carries a whip, starts to shout at a group of CHINESE WORKERS who are loading a wagon with debris.

FOREMAN
Get on with it, you lazy bastards! No, not like this. How many times do I have to tell you ...

BUFORD has almost reached the office, he is sweating profusely. The BOYS are giggling.

BUFORD
Gracias, boys. Here is what I promised you.

He pulls out some coins and hands each of them one.

BUFORD (cont'd)
Go on now. And be blessed.

The BOYS squeal with delight, eyeing their prizes, turning the coins in the sun. They run away.

EXT. RAILROAD OFFICE -- DAY

BUFORD walks to the RR Office. When he approaches it, he sees a GUARD sitting outside the door. The guard is dressed in a white uniform and he is sitting under a gigantic mosquito net which surrounds him like a small tent. A loaded gun stands next to him, plus a box of ammunition.

BUFORD
Good day, sir. I'm Father Jonathan White, from England, and I was told to see the head master of the company.

GUARD, looking at BUFORD. He fishes a thin cigar from his pocket and lights it. He blows out the smoke and squints his eyes.

GUARD
They even go under your net, damn little bloodsuckers... Head master? Head master is quaint. Reminds me of school.

He laughs and blows smoke.

GUARD
We call him "Boss" around here.
(pointing to the door)
Go right in.

BUFORD
Thank you. What's his name?

GUARD
Mr. Maddox.
(grinning).)
We call him Mr. Mad, though...when we don't call him Boss.

BUFORD
Thank you. He walks on.

GUARD
One advise: Make sure you have none of them bloodsuckers on your clothes when you get inside. He hates them.

BUFORD, who interrupted his walk, walks on, and in front of the door, he wipes his clothes. Then he knocks.

(CONTINUED)

CONTINUED:

BOSS MADDOX (O.S.)
Enter!

INT. RR OFFICE -- DAY

BUFORD enters the room and quickly closes the door behind him. The room is kept dark. BOSS MADDOX is bent over a table on which lie sketches, maps, papers.

BUFORD
Mr. Maddox, my name is Father White.
I came here to...

BOSS MADDOX, looking up from his papers and maps.

BOSS MADDOX
Delighted, Father ...White, you said?

BUFORD is walking towards the table, stretching out his hand.

BUFORD
From England.

BOSS MADDOX is grabbing BUFORD'S hand and shakes it.

BOSS MADDOX
Delighted, Father White. Have a seat.

He points to a couple of chairs in the corner. Both men walk over there and sit down.

BOSS MADDOX (cont'd)
May I offer you something to drink?
Juice, water, coconut milk?

BUFORD
Some water would be fine. It is hot
today.

BOSS MADDOX
(laughing)
I see you are new. Hot it is, indeed,
and we haven't had summer yet. How
may I help you.

BUFORD
Well, I was sent from the Church,
from Oxford in England, to come here
and ...

(CONTINUED)

CONTINUED:

BOSS MADDOX
(interrupting)
... you probably heard of Father McKenzie...?

BUFORD
Yes, I heard. Terrible, isn't it? How can people do such a thing?

BOSS MADDOX
(surprised)
I guess this was his way of saying "good bye" to us.

BUFORD
(confused)
"Good bye"? He must have suffered tremendously... at that tree... wrapped around it...

BOSS MADDOX is getting up, fetching a bottle of water, pouring himself and BUFORD a drink.

BOSS MADDOX
I'm not quite sure what you mean, Father White.

BUFORD
(confused)
I was told, Father McKenzie... he was killed by natives, wasn't he? His intestines ... wrapped around a tree...

BOSS MADDOX
(laughing out loud)
Who told you that story?

BUFORD
An Indian woman, in that house, where Father McKenzie used to live. Now there lives Father McKenzie's assistant. A Mr. Chester.

BOSS MADDOX
(dismissive)
Oh that old drunk. She told you that?
(He laughs.)
Oh no! No, no, no. That's not what happened to McKenzie.
(He laughs again.)
Far from it...No, Father McKenzie left us very suddenly. Very suddenly.
(MORE)

(CONTINUED)

CONTINUED:

BOSS MADDOX (cont'd)
And with a lot of gold, and a lot of money, and a lot of girls.

BUFORD
(astounded)
Beg your pardon?

BOSS MADDOX
Oh yes, my words are true. He took off one day, after he had "collected" money from every soul in town, including a large sum from this company, then he and his gang robbed men of their gold nuggets who had just returned from California, and to make things worse, he took all 20 girls with him.
(beat)
Fine girls, all French from New Orleans, some even from Europe... And that fellow who was wrapped around a tree, that was his right hand in the heist. A certain Mulroy. Nasty bastard. Wanted too much.

BUFORD
And where is fath.. I mean McKenzie now?

BOSS MADDOX
In Panama City. The last thing I heard was, he runs a brothel, owns a liquor store, a hotel, and has a mule business. I guess he quit his faith...

BUFORD is sipping from his water for the first time.

BUFORD
Well,...

BOSS MADDOX
Father White, if I may give you an advice. Don't believe everything you hear. Don't even believe everything you see. Here in the jungle, reality is different from what you are used to. After some time, you'll understand and hopefully accept it. Because if you don't, you'll go mad.

(CONTINUED)

CONTINUED:

BUFORD
What, Mr. Maddox, am I supposed to do?

BOSS MADDOX
You can work for us. The company is building a hospital, and there we need a man, like you, who can nurse the spirit and the soul of patients. Because we have a lot of sick and dying men out here. A lot, and only 10 miles of tracks are laid.
(beat)
And 40 more to go.

BACK TO:

INT. SEEDY HOTEL ROOM -- PANAMA CITY -- DAY

MARIE is feeding BUFORD who is still in bed.

BUFORD
Hmm, very tasty that ham. Where did you buy it?

MARIE
At the market. It's just one block down from here.

BUFORD
Did you get also some opium?

MARIE
Later. I met someone, he can get it for me.

BUFORD
Good. Now, tell me something about yourself. How did you end up here, in Panama?

MARIE
(hesitant)
So they hired you then, at the Railroad?

BUFORD
Yes. They started me at the hospital which was still under construction, in some way.

CONTINUED:

MARIE
I don't understand.

BUFORD
The Railroad Company did not have enough money at that time therefore, the hospital was only a barrack with a couple of beds. But I met the hospital's physician, Dr. Rubber, who showed me around... But tell me, Marie, how did you get here?

MARIE
Maybe later. You pay me to listen to your story. I don't have the money to pay you to listen to mine.

BUFORD
(looking at her)
Maybe I would listen anyway.

MARIE
How long did you work for the hospital?

BUFORD
For how long? I don't remember. One month, two, three...time dissolves under your very eyes here in Panama. One hour in the midday sun seems like an eternity. And at night, when the birds cry out their pain, and the apes stare at you from behind the bushes with red-hot eyes, you have lost all feelings for reality.

MARIE
More ham?

She offers him the plate with the cut slices of ham.

BUFORD
(taking a slice)
I never thought that time can be so fluid and that my sense of reality could be so questionable. Or maybe it isn't at all! Maybe my senses are real and sound...it's just the world that's strange.

MARIE
Or maybe it's the opium playing games with your head.
(MORE)

(CONTINUED)

CONTINUED:

MARIE (cont'd)
So, they hired you and you began to work in the hospital. How was your first day?

BUFORD
My first day?
(sarcastic)
My first day...

FLASH BACK TO:

EXT. CONSTRUCTION SITE OF RAILROAD COMPANY -- A BARRACK -- DAY

BUFORD meets the scientist, DR. RUBBER (50, glasses), who is conducting research and wants to find out which race can survive the harsh working conditions best. He has established a sort of "Skeleton Museum" where he keeps skeletons of men. These skeletons are standing upright in groups together and are classified according to their nationality and race. Buford is approaching Dr. Rubber's office, knocking at his door.

BUFORD
Dr. Rubber?

DR. RUBBER (V.O.)
Come on in.

INT. DR. RUBBER'S OFFICE -- DAY

BUFORD enters the room which is pleasantly cooled by ice.

BUFORD
Good morning, Dr. Rubber. Sorry I'm a bit late but today it is especially hot and humid. I am Father Jonathan White, from England.

The men shake hands, DR. RUBBER points to a chair.

DR. RUBBER
Please have a seat. No need to excuse. Here on the strip--the workers call it "Hell Strip", I hear--time has its own reality. There is real time, and there is felt time.

BUFORD
Indeed. And felt time seems always at least twice as long as real time.

(CONTINUED)

CONTINUED:

DR. RUBBER
Unless you are sick with yellow fever or malaria, then felt time is like an eternity.

BUFORD
(clearing his throat)
I hear that you are conducting research, Dr. Rubber, that you want to find out how long humans can survive these harsh working conditions.

DR. RUBBER
That's correct. I have come to very interesting conclusions which will advance medicine a great deal.

BUFORD
Perhaps you could enlighten me a bit.

DR. RUBBER
Certainly, certainly. Well, we would have to go outside. Please follow me.

DR. RUBBER gets up from his chair, fetches an ice pickle and cuts a small piece of ice which he puts into his mouth.

DR. RUBBER (cont'd)
Do you want some too, Father White? It keeps you cool a bit.

BUFORD
No thank you.

DR. RUBBER
Very well, then.

EXT. CONSTRUCTION SITE OF RAILROAD COMPANY -- DAY

They both leave the office and step outside. The sun is brutally hot. DR. RUBBER walks to a little hill from which one has a panoramic view on the scenery. Hundreds of MEN are laboring at the railroad tracks. Most of them sunk in the mud and swamp up to their hips. One can hear constant cursing in several languages. SUPERVISORS, all are dressed in white uniforms with hats on and whistles hanging around their necks, shout instructions.

(CONTINUED)

CONTINUED:

DR. RUBBER
(stretching out his arms)
As you can see, here are men at work.
(he points to them)
This fresh load came yesterday. They are all Irish. The last load of Irish men we had, back in July, lasted exactly for one week.

BUFORD
What do you mean by "lasted"?

DR. RUBBER
(he looks at Buford)
What do I mean? I'll show you. Follow me.

Both men leave the hill and DR. RUBBER takes BUFORD to a barrack. Dr Rubber stops in front of the door and he turns to Buford.

DR. RUBBER (cont'd)
Now, I want you to breathe as little as possible! And most of all: don't touch anything. If a man stretches out his hand to grab you, kick it away with your boots. Don't let them touch you! Understand?

BUFORD
Yes, but...

DR. RUBBER
You'll see in a minute.

EXT./INT. BARRACK

They enter the barrack. A hellish stench engulfs both men as they walk into the middle of the room. Left and right one can see bunk beds with MEN lying on them, moaning, shaking with fever, throwing up, wincing in pain and so on. BUFORD is horrified by the sight and puts his handkerchief in front of his mouth and nose.

DR. RUBBER
(shouting, pointing to the bunk beds)
This is the "Rotting Room." These men completed "Phase I" and are now in "Phase II."

(CONTINUED)

CONTINUED:

BUFORD
"Phase I"?

DR. RUBBER
I just showed you. "Phase I" is the phase where they are still working.

He points to the door. Then he points to this room.

DR. RUBBER (cont'd)
And this is "Phase II. Let's go. I want to show you "Phase III."

INT./EXT. CONSTRUCTION SITE OF RAILROAD COMPANY

Both men leave the barrack and step outside. They gasp for fresh air.

DR. RUBBER
Now you understand why we call this the "Rotting Room," don't you?

BUFORD
(nodding)
There is nothing one can do for these poor souls?

DR. RUBBER
Of course, there is. If you wish, you can do your kind of work and ease their spiritual pain. It's up to you! Now let me show you "Phase III."

DR. RUBBER walks with BUFORD to the "Skeleton Museum." Groups of skeletons are standing around, all are labeled according to race and nationality. Dr. Rubber is noticing with professional enthusiasm that his demonstrations have had their desired effect.

DR. RUBBER (cont'd)
(proud)
This is "Phase III." Here,
(he points to a group nearby)
these are Germans and one or two Danes. Not bad workers, but after a few weeks in the swamp ... I had to put them here. And here...

He points to a group of skeletons that are much smaller in stature.

(CONTINUED)

CONTINUED:

DR. RUBBER
...we have Chinese men. Good workers. But they can't work well in the swamp. Too short, you know. They drown easily. And to pull them out of the swamp is like catching jellyfish. But here...

He points to a small group of strong and tall skeletons.

DR. RUBBER (cont'd)
...these are the best! They are from West Africa. Slow at work, but tough. They don't mind the heat, they are resistant against fever,and best of all: they don't get paid...in short: first rate! That's all I can say: First Rate.

BUFORD
And why are they here, if they best survive the conditions?

DR. RUBBER is pointing to the group of the West Africans.

DR. RUBBER
Shot by the guards. Did not follow orders quickly enough!

BUFORD
Shot? Weren't they workers too?

DR. RUBBER
Workers, yes, but slaves. No pay, just food and shelter. But I should not forget to show you our newest scientific project. Please follow along.

Both men walk to another barrack.

BUFORD
There is more?

DR. RUBBER
You see, men are dying so fast and in such large numbers that we can't bury them fast enough. You might have seen a corpse here or there on your way to the construction site, haven't you?
(MORE)

(CONTINUED)

CONTINUED:

DR. RUBBER (cont'd)
(without waiting for
an answer)
Usually, the alligators take care of
it within an hour or two. But have
you seen how fat they've become?
Nowadays, one can step right in front
of them and touch their noses ... if
one desires to do so. They are too
lazy to snap.

BUFORD
No, I haven't tried it yet.

Both men stop in front of the barrack.

DR. RUBBER
Here we are. Do you notice that acrid
smell?

EXT./INT. BARRACK -- THE "PICKLE ROOM"

He opens the door and they enter the barrack. BUFORD puts his handkerchief over his nose and mouth again.

BUFORD
What smell is that? It burns my
throat.

DR. RUBBER
You'll see.

He leads BUFORD to a row of wooden boxes. There are about 50 of them lined up.

DR. RUBBER (cont'd)
Have a look.

He points to one of the boxes.

DR. RUBBER (cont'd)
Here they are.

BUFORD bends over and looks into the box. He jerks back immediately. Bewildered he looks at DR. RUBBER.

DR. RUBBER (cont'd)
(nodding)
I admit, they do look a bit greenish,
but at least they don't spoil.

BUFORD
Why do they look that way?

(CONTINUED)

CONTINUED:

DR. RUBBER
(demonstrative)
We are in the "Pickle Room". The corpses are put into a mixture of vinegar, salt and sulfate....it's like ... it's like pickling cucumbers to turn them into gherkins.

BUFORD
You mean, in those boxes there are pickled corpses?

DR. RUBBER
(nodding with satisfaction)
Indeed, there are. It took me several weeks to come up with a mixture that keeps the corpse balanced in an acceptable state of conservation. You see, if the solution is too strong, which means too acidic, the corpse will shrink and becomes leather-like... You don't want that!

BUFORD
I guess not.

DR. RUBBER
If the solution is too mild, though, the skin and the flesh underneath do spoil... slowly, very slowly, it takes some time... but nevertheless, they spoil... and you don't want that either.

BUFORD
Not really...

DR. RUBBER
You see, the skin becomes kind of soapy and then the corpse is difficult to handle. You have no idea...it's like holding on to a rotten fish. Often you think you finally got hold of the corpse when you realize that you are only holding a piece of flesh in your hands. Rotten flesh tears very easily, you see, and before you know it, you have a mess lying in front of you... And of course, the stench...unbearable. Especially when you made the mistake of grabbing the guts.

(CONTINUED)

CONTINUED:

BUFORD
No question, of course.
(swallowing)
And what is the purpose of ... doing all this?

DR. RUBBER
(standing proud)
We sell the pickled corpses to hospitals and universities in Europe and the United States where they are used for research. Besides, it pays for our hospital.

BUFORD
Research?

DR. RUBBER
Yes, of course. We have to increase our knowledge of the human body, don't we. Besides, our pickled friends are much more useful than the ones you have to dig from the graves. As you can imagine by now, the unearthed fellows, untreated with a solution, dissolve easily under your hands. They lie there... and you suppose, it is safe to pull their arm or poke their gooey chest, but no... after a mere five weeks in the ground, all you see is little red-eyed worms munching their way up to the light, looking at you with amazement...

BUFORD
I guess so. It's...I have never really thought about that, I suppose.

DR. RUBBER
Well, we all learn new things every day, don't we. But regardless whether they are pickled, lie underground, or stand as skeletons in the bright sun, they will all face their maker in the end, won't they.

BUFORD
Yes, sir, they will. To the Lord there is no difference. He loves them all, pickled, bony or otherwise.

(CONTINUED)

CONTINUED:

DR. RUBBER
That's good to know, Father White.
Good to know. Now let's leave this
room and get some fresh air. My skin
begins to feel like a raisin.
(laughs)
This way, please.

Both men leave the barrack.

INT. RR OFFICE -- DAY

BUFORD is sitting in MADDOX'S OFFICE. They sip water.

BOSS MADDOX
It comes down to this: the more
corpses we sell to Europe and the
United States, the faster can we
finish our own hospital. Did Dr.
Rubber give you a tour?

BUFORD
Indeed, he did. First he showed me
the "Rotting Room" and then the
"Pickle Room."

BOSS MADDOX
Good, old Dr. Rubber. Always so eager
to show his research. As I said, we
need to sell more corpses to get the
money flowing. Meanwhile, I have a
job for you.

BUFORD
What can I do for you?

BOSS MADDOX
It's a delicate matter, really, and I
need your full cooperation.

BUFORD
I do what I can.

BOSS MADDOX
A prominent Lady from Baltimore is
visiting us. Mrs. Elizabeth Lennox.
She is the widow of Mr. Herbert
Lennox, an entrepreneur who invested
into railroads... but unfortunately
died, falling off a horse.
(MORE)

(CONTINUED)

CONTINUED:

BOSS MADDOX (cont'd)
She wants to see whether her company could invest into the Panama railroad we are building. She wants to stay here for a day or two and then travel across the isthmus to Panama City.

BUFORD
Travel? Through the jungle and the swamp?

BOSS MADDOX
(nervous)
I know, Father White, I know. But I couldn't talk her out of it. She thinks it is a little trip through the forest with exotic birds and flowers and the occasional monkey swinging from tree to tree.

BUFORD
Is there a road through the jungle?

BOSS MADDOX
Yes, kind of a road... but people travel it daily. Especially all the men who come back from California with gold in their pockets. And all the ones who are on their way to El Dorado. It's called the "Yankee Trail". Lots of bars, casinos, and plenty of hotels, and you know, other establishments.

BUFORD
How does Lady Lennox travel?

BOSS MADDOX
Well, you two will use mules, and of course a native will come along as a guide.

BUFORD
You two?

BOSS MADDOX
I hope, I can count on you, Father White. It is very important, very.

BUFORD
(alarmed)
What am I supposed to do?

CONTINUED:

BOSS MADDOX
You pick her up at the harbor in Colon. Then you bring her here, and after I spoke with her, you accompany her to Panama City.

BUFORD
(opening his collar)
And then?

BOSS MADDOX
You return by yourself, because Lady Lennox is continuing her journey by steamer to San Francisco.

BUFORD
And when is she arriving in Colon?

BOSS MADDOX
Tomorrow morning. With the "Nicaragua."

EXT. COLON HARBOR -- MORNING

The steamer "Nicaragua" is moored a hundred yards away from the landing. On board about fifty PASSENGERS wait with their luggage to go on land. But instead of boats that would bring them to shore, TEN INDIAN MEN who were standing at the pier are now wading into the shallow water. The Indians are only wearing loin cloths. The passengers eye the approaching Indians with wonderment.

PASSENGER 1
(laughing and shouting)
Is this the welcome committee?

Others laugh also and point to the INDIANS who come closer to the ship.

PASSENGER 2
What's missing is some music!

More laughter. The CHILDREN especially find the approaching INDIANS funny, some are afraid though.

CHILD 1
Mummy, are they going to hurt us?

MUMMY
No, dear. They are friendly.

(CONTINUED)

CONTINUED:

CHILD 1
What are they doing?

MUMMY
I really don't know, dear. Maybe it's a local custom we don't know about.

On the pier, a CROWD has assembled and a MARCHING BAND is lining up. This band is colorfully dressed in red, blue, orange, pink garments, resembling costumes from an opera. On top of their heads, the band's members wear feathers. The CONDUCTOR is beginning a popular song. MERCHANTS are selling watermelons, bananas, coco nuts, hats, clothes, and so on. There is a festive atmosphere at the harbor. MORE PEOPLE on board wonder what this is all about. Some wave to the people at the pier who wave back. Meanwhile the INDIANS have come closer to the ship. The first to arrive stand up to their hips in the water. They stretch out their arms, then point to their shoulders, then they turn around and show their backs. Some PASSENGERS think this is a form of local greeting and also stretch out their arms, then turn around and show their backs.

The INDIANS who see this shake their heads and point with their hands and outstretched fingers to their own shoulders, mimicking they would carry the passengers on their backs. The PASSENGERS, not understanding, do the same. There is laughter, some passengers start to sing; in the background the marching band is walking up and down the pier, blowing their brass instruments. Some merchant opens a cage and a hundred colorful birds fly into the air. The CAPTAIN of the ship walks down to the waiting passengers all of whom are now waving and shouting to the Indians and the folks on the pier.

CAPTAIN
Ladies and Gentlemen. Welcome to Colon, Panama. Perhaps I should explain. Our steamer, the "Nicaragua" can't move closer to shore for the waters are too shallow this time of the year. And since we have reached a foreign land which still is unburdened by the weight of civilization, the mode of transportation is a bit different from what you might expect. Instead of rowing boats that would take you to land, these Porters you see standing in the water will carry you and your luggage. Let me assure you this is a safe but in some cases bit wet journey.

(CONTINUED)

CONTINUED:

The PASSENGERS look at the CAPTAIN in utter disbelief. After the first shock is over, some start to crack jokes.

PASSENGER
The captain had too much rum for lunch.

OTHER PASSENGER
I always wanted to ride an Indian.

THIRD PASSENGER
Panama: Here I come!

CAPTAIN
We will have small ladders lowered into the sea. At the end, a Porter will wait and you climb onto his shoulder. He then will carry you safely to land.

PASSENGER
What about my luggage?

CAPTAIN
Your luggage will be carried by a second Water Porter.

A LADY
But Captain. How can a lady mount the shoulders of a savage without compromising herself?

CAPTAIN
It can be done, My Lady, it can be done. Think of mounting a horse, and then hold on to the man's long hair like you would to the mane of a stallion.

A SECOND LADY
But my undergarment will touch the neck of a man. This is impossible.

CAPTAIN
These men are completely de-sensitized from the neck down.

SECOND LADY
(snappy)
De-sensitized? But my undergarment is not!

(CONTINUED)

CONTINUED:

Some PASSENGERS think by now that this is part of the Caribbean adventure they have embarked and walk down the ladders that have been lowered into the water. Then they mount the shoulder of a PORTER who walks away with them. The first ones who do this are cheered on the passengers waiting on board. It all seems now to be a jolly affair and is taken lightly. Some MALE PASSENGERS are even hopping onto the shoulders and a few fall off into the water which is accompanied by laughs and cheers. Some LADIES turn this into a difficult and comical affair. There is a lot of shrieking and laughing, shouting and yelling. But one by one the passengers are carried to shore where the band is playing and the already safely arrived passengers clap their hands whenever another passengers arrives. BUFORD is standing at the pier, looking out for LADY LENNOX. When the first women arrive on land, he shouts out, waving his arms:

BUFORD
Lady Lennox? Lady Lennox?

The first couple of times, he has no luck but a few moments later, one of the WOMEN who is still atop a PORTER points behind her.

WOMAN
Lady Lennox is behind me.

BUFORD squints his eyes. Then he sees a WOMAN all dressed in white being carried towards him. When the woman arrives and is lowered to the ground by the PORTER, Buford walks toward her. LADY LENNOX 35, good looking, tall.

BUFORD
Lady Lennox.

LADY LENNOX
(straightening her clothes)
Yees?

BUFORD
(nervous)
Welcome, Lady Lennox. I'm Father White. I am here to welcome you to Panama and to accompany you to the Railroad Office. Mr. Maddox sent me.

LADY LENNOX, looking at BUFORD, then looking at the BAND, the MERCHANTS, the CROWD.

LADY LENNOX
Are you for real or are you part of this carnival?

(CONTINUED)

CONTINUED:

BUFORD
(a bit indignant)
Of course, I am for real, Lady Lennox. Mr. Maddox sent me. I will guide you to his office. My coach is waiting over there.

BUFORD picks up her luggage, then he is seeing her to the mule-drawn coach. He helps her in, after he has stowed away the bags. He swings on the driver's seat, and cheers the mule on. But the mule doesn't move. He tries several times but has no luck. Finally, he climbs down and takes the mule by the rope, then he walks alongside the mule and the coach moves on.

BACK TO:

INT. SEEDY HOTEL ROOM -- PANAMA CITY -- DAY

BUFORD is lying in bed again, smoking a pipe after he and MARIE had lunch. Marie is sitting by the window which is half open and looks outside.

MARIE
I bet she was a pretty woman, your Lady Lennox. Pretty and with lots of money.

BUFORD
(blowing out smoke)
Pretty she was but also demanding. Nothing was right. She wanted this and that and everything all at once. That night, after she and Maddox had talked business, she requested that I go with her to her hotel downtown.

MARIE
And I bet, you did.

BUFORD
Yes, I had no choice.

MARIE
Of course not. How can you have a choice when a beautiful and rich woman asks you up to her room.

She gets up and walks around the table, then she walks up to BUFORD'S bed. MARIE sits down on the edge of the bed.

(CONTINUED)

CONTINUED:

MARIE (cont'd)
You probably slept with her, right?

BUFORD
Slept with her?
(laughs)
Oh no. Not at all.

FLASH BACK TO:

INT. ROOM -- HOTEL DOWNTOWN -- COLON -- EVENING

LADY LENNOX and BUFORD who is carrying her luggage are entering the room. Buford sets the bags down and is about to leave.

LADY LENNOX
(looking at Buford)
You are not leaving, aren't you?

BUFORD
(at the door)
Yes, ... is there something else?

LADY LENNOX
You must be joking. Leaving me here, alone, in the middle of the night, in this ...forsaken place.... Here,
(she hands Buford a small towel)
chase the mosquitoes out first. And when that is done, I want you to sleep right there.

She points to the bed.

BUFORD
But Lady Lennox, I can't sleep in the same bed with you...

LADY LENNOX
Not in the bed...what are you thinking! I want you to sleep right there.

She walks to the bed and points to the floor.

LADY LENNOX
Right there.

CONTINUED:

BUFORD
You want me to sleep on the floor, in front of your bed?

LADY LENNOX
(cold)
Father White, where else? There is no other bed in this room!

BACK TO:

INT. SEEDY HOTEL ROOM -- PANAMA CITY -- DAY

MARIE is laughing out loud.

MARIE
So you had to sleep on the floor? Next to her bed? With the cockroaches?

She laughs again.

BUFORD
And that was only the beginning of the journey with Lady Lennox.

FLASH BACK TO:

EXT. RR HEADQUARTERS -- COLON -- EARLY MORNING

BUFORD waits outside the railroad office, preparing three mules for the journey to Panama City. Although early in the morning, the heat is oppressive. He fastens the saddlebags. He looks around for the native, Maddox has promised to come along, but the native is nowhere to be seen. A moment later. LADY LENNOX appears, all fancily dressed in lace, carrying a parasol. She looks cheery and upbeat.

BUFORD
Good morning, Lady Lennox. I hope you're well rested. It will be a long day.

LADY LENNOX
I know it will. And good morning to you too. Everything is packed, I see. Will we have enough water?

BUFORD
It should last till the next stop.

(CONTINUED)

CONTINUED:

LADY LENNOX
And where is that?

BUFORD
Somewhere on the way, not far.

LADY LENNOX
I trust you, Father White. After all, God is with us.

BUFORD
He is not only with us, Lady Lennox, he is always one step ahead of us.

LADY LENNOX
Well, then we have nothing to fear.

BUFORD helps LADY LENNOX get settled on the mule. He mounts his own mule and looks around. The native still is nowhere to be seen.

BUFORD
The native, Mr. Maddox promised, hasn't shown up yet. Shall we keep waiting?

LADY LENNOX
(looking around)
If he can't be punctual, he won't be of any use to us anyway. Let's go.

BUFORD
Very well then.

They ride on.

EXT. JUNGLE -- YANKEE TRAIL -- DAY

To the left and right, there is abundant jungle vegetation. Some MEN are passing by, riding mules, leaving them behind. Birds are screeching, there are strange calling sounds by unseen animals. Some hushed movement is heard among the leaves. LADY LENNOX looks about in wonderment. She is riding ahead, followed by BUFORD.

LADY LENNOX
(smiling)
Isn't that absolutely beautiful! I wish we had something like this in Baltimore to retreat for the weekend.

CONTINUED:

She points to the left, where there is a colorful bird sitting on a branch; she turns around:

LADY LENNOX (cont'd)
Did you see that? Do you know its name?

BUFORD, a bit embarrassed because he really doesn't know the local fauna, makes up the name.

BUFORD
The locals, I believe, call it the Macadoo.

LADY LENNOX is pointing to another bird sitting on the right hand side.

LENNOX
And what do you call that?

BUFORD
(still embarrassed)
I think this is his cousin, the Cacadoo.

LADY LENNOX looks a bit disbelievingly and suspiciously at BUFORD who tries to hide the smirk on his face. Then she points to another bird in front of them and says:

LADY LENNOX
Well, I see, this must be then his distant cousin, whose name I'm sure you know, too.

BUFORD
Here, you got me. I only know it is from the same family. But I can't recall its name.

LADY LENNOX
If it is the same family, it must be a "something-doo."

BUFORD
You are absolutely ... true.

LADY LENNOX
(muttering, smiling)
Well, good for ... you!

BACK TO:

INT. SEEDY HOTEL ROOM -- PANAMA CITY -- DAY

BUFORD is sitting on his bed, propped up by cushions against the wall. MARIE is sitting next to him on a chair.

BUFORD
So we traveled through the jungle on the "Yankee Trail", one mule-step at a time. The heat became intolerable. At noon time, we both were exhausted and needed a rest in the shade.

FLASH BACK TO:

EXT. JUNGLE -- YANKEE TRAIL -- DAY

BUFORD and LADY LENNOX are sitting under a tree, resting.

LADY LENNOX
So tell me, Father White. What brought you to Panama?

BUFORD
I want to bring the word of God to the natives here.

LADY LENNOX
So, the word of God. What does your God say about human desire?

BUFORD
(taken aback)
Of course, he condemns it.

LADY LENNOX
Of course.

LADY LENNOX stretches out under the tree. BUFORD is eyeing her. He inches a bit closer, until both lie next to each other. Buford is touching very lightly Lennox' hand, when suddenly TWO MEN ON HORSES pass by, then stop. They look frantically around as if they were searching for someone. The two men stop close to where Buford and LADY LENNOX are. Both duck down in the grass. Then the two men, rough-looking cowboys, take three bags which seem heavy and put them into a tree trunk. They mark the trunk with a chalk, and then they leave. Lennox and Buford raise their heads to see whether the men are gone.

BUFORD
They are gone.

(CONTINUED)

CONTINUED:

LADY LENNOX
Are you sure?

BUFORD gets up and looks around. Then he walks to the tree trunk where the bags are hidden. He takes one and opens it.

BUFORD
(whistling through his teeth)
Look what I found...

LADY LENNOX walks up to him.

LADY LENNOX
What is it?

BUFORD
Opium.

BUFORD opens the two other bags.

BUFORD
And more opium...

Lady Lennox and BUFORD both look at each other.

BACK TO:

INT. SEEDY HOTEL ROOM -- PANAMA CITY -- DAY

BUFORD reaches for the pipe but MARIE moves it away.

BUFORD
Well, if you don't let me have the pipe, what can I have instead...?

There is a moment of silence. MARIE looks at BUFORD with a stone-cold expression on her face.

MARIE
You'll see.

BUFORD is occupied with the pipe, but when the words sink in, he looks at MARIE.

BUFORD
What do you mean?

MARIE'S expression relaxes. She smiles.

MARIE
Let me help you with that pipe.

(CONTINUED)

CONTINUED:

She takes the pipe and prepares it, then she gives it back to BUFORD.

MARIE (cont'd)
This is especially good opium. Very strong. Be careful. So what did you do with all that opium?

BUFORD
We took it with us to Panama City. Lady Lennox said, it would be a waste to leave it in the jungle... And so we did.

MARIE
You weren't afraid that the men would come and look for you?

BUFORD
I was, but the lady wasn't. She said, they haven't seen us. So how would they know?

MARIE
And then, what happened next?

FLASH BACK TO:

EXT. A STOP-OVER ON THE YANKEE TRAIL -- EVENING

BUFORD and LADY LENNOX enter a small place on the trail. It consists of mostly bars, a few hotels, a casino and a brothel. Many MEN walk about, mostly drunk, some shoot guns in the air. In front of the brothel, there is a line of MEN waiting.

INT. HOTEL LOBBY -- EVENING

LENNOX AND BUFORD rent a room in a hotel, and take their luggage and the three bags to their room.

INT. HOTEL ROOM -- EVENING

BUFORD is putting the bags with the opium into a corner. LADY LENNOX sits on the bed.

BUFORD
What are we going to do with the opium?

(CONTINUED)

CONTINUED:

LADY LENNOX
We are going to sell it.

BUFORD
Sell it? To whom?

LADY LENNOX
The Panama Railroad Company.

BUFORD
Why to them?

LADY LENNOX looks at BUFORD.

LADY LENNOX
Are you really that naive or do you just pretend to be?

BUFORD
Enlighten me.

LADY LENNOX
You have seen them, right?

BUFORD
Seen what?

LADY LENNOX
The Chinese workers... there are hundreds of Chinese...they are hooked on opium... they need it every day.

BUFORD
How do you know that?

LADY LENNOX
Look, the English trade with China but import more tea from China then they can sell wool clothes or steam engines or God knows what to them. So, in order to make up for the trade deficit, they sell the Chinese opium which they harvest in India, which is their colony... It is done by the East India Company...You are English, and you don't know that?

BUFORD
I never looked at it that way.

LADY LENNOX
So we sell the opium to the RR company, and everybody is happy.

CONTINUED:

BUFORD
And who is going to sell it to the RR Company?

LADY LENNOX
You do! But not directly to them, we will find someone here who will.

BUFORD
But why should I sell it...?

LADY LENNOX
Because, being a priest is a good disguise, isn't it?

BACK TO:

INT. SEEDY HOTEL ROOM -- PANAMA CITY -- DAY

BUFORD takes a draw from the pipe and smiles.

BUFORD
And so it came to pass... That evening I went to one of the bars and met a guy to whom I sold the stuff...

FLASH BACK TO:

EXT./INT. YANKEE TRAIL -- BAR -- NIGHT

BUFORD is entering a crowded bar but despite his priest outfit, he is drawing little attention. The room is full of SAILORS, COWBOYS, PIRATES, GENTLEMEN, PROSTITUTES... The bar is loud, people drink and laugh. Money is flowing. MEN have just come back from California where they had dug for gold. Some were lucky, others are desperate. Some SHADY CHARACTERS eye the ones who have their pockets full of money. Buford stands in the background, surveying the crowd. He picks one smart-looking, well-dressed MAN, 30, who in turn is scanning the crowd. Their eyes meet. Buford walks outside.

EXT. BAR -- NIGHT

PEOPLE are walking up and down the strip, some arm in arm, other stagger. Here and there, MEN have passed out and lie on the sidewalk. In some house entrances, PROSTITUTES stand. BUFORD leans against a post and looks at the clear night sky. The noise of the jungle is faintly present. The air is full of the droning sound of cicadas.

(CONTINUED)

CONTINUED:

After a few moments, the smart-looking MAN is stepping outside the bar. He sees Buford but remains at some distance. Buford looks at him.

BUFORD
Nice night.

STRANGER
Indeed.

BUFORD
On the way to Colon or to Panama City?

STRANGER
Colon. And you?

BUFORD
Panama City. Then to San Francisco. Out of here.

STRANGER
Can't blame you. Just coming from there.

The STRANGER looks at BUFORD and steps a bit closer.

STRANGER
What is a priest doing in this place?

BUFORD
There are many lost souls to be found.

STRANGER
I guess, you are right.

The STRANGER turns and wants to walk away.

BUFORD
Many lost souls who suffer because they do not get what they want...

STRANGER
(turning around, coming closer)
And what do these lost souls want?

BUFORD
Unfortunately, they can't be helped, their suffering only can be eased.

(CONTINUED)

CONTINUED:

STRANGER
Why is that?

BUFORD
They already sold their souls to the Devil.

STRANGER
And...?

BUFORD
God can only provide them with a remedy that eases their suffering, if you know what I mean.

STRANGER
I am getting there...

BUFORD
They are Chinese who work at the Railroad in the most horrible of conditions. Laying tracks in the swamp, standing up to their hips in water, and then there are alligators, snakes, mosquitoes, and ruthless supervisors...

STRANGER
And their suffering is relieved by smoking?

BUFORD
Yes.

STRANGER
How many suffer?

BUFORD
Several hundred.

STRANGER
And they all can be helped?

BUFORD
Yes, and more.

STRANGER
I think my duty as a Christian requires me to offer relief.

(CONTINUED)

CONTINUED:

BUFORD
Especially in view of the fact that the remedy grows in God's own nature...

STRANGER
Especially in view of that fact. And how much has grown on God's field?

BUFORD
Three bags full.

STRANGER
Well, it might take an hour to come up with the funds. But I see no problem.

BUFORD
I'll see you in an hour then.

BACK TO:

INT. SEEDY HOTEL ROOM -- PANAMA CITY -- DAY

BUFORD draws a puff from the pipe.

BUFORD
And so it happened. I met the guy an hour later, we exchanged the goods, and I delivered the money to Lady Lennox.

MARIE
And what happened next?

BUFORD
Well, Lady Lennox was very nice to me when I showed up with the money.

MARIE
I knew you slept with her...

FLASH BACK TO:

INT. YANKEE TRAIL -- HOTEL ROOM -- NIGHT

BUFORD is entering the hotel room where LADY LENNOX is waiting. She looks at him and he smiles, lifting up a bag which is full of money.

(CONTINUED)

CONTINUED:

BUFORD
Everything went smoothly. Here it is.

He throws the money on the bed. LADY LENNOX opens the bag and looks into it.

BUFORD (cont'd)
Five thousand Dollars. And some gold nuggets.

LADY LENNOX
Good work. Maybe...
(she points to the bed)
maybe tonight, you don't have to sleep on the floor.

BACK TO:

INT. SEEDY HOTEL ROOM -- PANAMA CITY -- DAY

BUFORD smokes some more.

BUFORD
Of course, I had set some of the opium and money aside for myself, but I can't believe what a fool I was.

MARIE
Why, what happened?

BUFORD
So, she basically invites me to bed...and when I get ready to join her, she says that I should clean up first in the bathroom.

FLASH BACK TO:

INT. YANKEE TRAIL -- HOTEL ROOM -- NIGHT

BUFORD is joining LENNOX on the bed. He starts to caress her and he wants to kiss her.

LADY LENNOX
(laughing)
Before we get any further, you need to wash up first. You smell like a bar and a brothel all rolled into one.

(CONTINUED)

CONTINUED:

BUFORD
Of course, my lady. I will come back shiny and sparkling clean.

BUFORD jumps up, happy, and whisks to the bathroom. He undresses, pours water into the bowl and begins to wash himself.

BACK TO:

INT. SEEDY HOTEL ROOM -- PANAMA CITY -- DAY

BUFORD is stoned and pauses when he speaks. MARIE watches him.

BUFORD
Of course, when I came back...she was gone. And the money, too! I looked for her in the bars that night, but to no avail. The lady was gone for good.

MARIE
Ohhh... I am so sorry...

BUFORD
Well...at least I had some of the opium which eased my pain... So I continued the next day to Panama City, and here I am. Broke and hooked.

MARIE
Life can be so cruel... here, have another puff. I scored some strong opium, it is laced with hashish. You'll need it.

BUFORD
And what is your story, Marie? Tell me. What is yours?

FLASH TO:

EXT. COMTE ETIENNE DE BELMONT ESTATE -- HONFLEUR (FRANCE)-- DAY (1849)

ETIENNE DE BELMONT, mid-thirties, handsome, and his daughter MARIE, 16, beautiful, are in a small rowing boat on the lake. It is summer, a blue sky, a few feather clouds, a soft breeze.

(CONTINUED)

CONTINUED:

De Belmont is rowing slowly, Marie has her eyes closed, dreaming, she is humming a melody. A blue heron is flying by.

DE BELMONT
Marie, look! A blue heron.

He stops rowing and points to the heron. MARIE opens her eyes and looks about. Then she sees it.

MARIE
Oh yes. How pretty.

Her FATHER continues to row.

DE BELMONT
Keep your eyes open, my love, and take it all in.

MARIE
(she looks at her father)
Daddy, must we go to England? I'd rather stay here.

DE BELMONT
(he looks away)
You'll like it there. Besides, it is time for you to explore the world.

MARIE
(agitated)
I heard in England they eat with their hands and they don't use perfume, and they wear funny hats, and that they don't speak French, and that...

DE BELMONT
(laughing, interrupting)
Marie, Marie... who told you all that? We will be among civilized people who use fork and knives, who wear perfume, imported from France, of course, and who speak a word or two of French.

MARIE
I don't like going to England!

BACK TO:

INT. SEEDY HOTEL ROOM -- PANAMA CITY -- DAY

MARIE gets up and fetches a glass of water. She drinks and looks at BUFORD.

MARIE
And a few weeks later, we arrived in England. He only wanted to stay for a week, but everything turned out different.

She drinks again.

MARIE
My father met his business partner, Mr. Rochester, who was an associate of the East India Company. I did not know then, that the East India Company traded in opium with China.

MARIE looks at BUFORD who inhales smoke again from the opium pipe. He looks detached.

BUFORD
I learned that from that wicked lady...Lennox

MARIE
And then one morning, my father left the hotel to meet Mr. Rochester...and he never returned.

BUFORD
What had happened?

MARIE
Well, Mr. Rochester came to see me later that day to inform me that my father had had a fatal accident and that his last wish was that he should take care of me.

BUFORD
I am so sorry, Marie.

MARIE
And that, Mr. Rochester did. He took care of me...

She sobs for a brief moment, then regains her composure.

BUFORD
How did he take care of you?

(CONTINUED)

CONTINUED:

MARIE
I don't want to talk about it. I hated it, and I hated Southampton, too.

BUFORD
(suddenly alert)
Southampton?

MARIE
Yes, Southampton...

BUFORD
(nervous)
Tell me, Marie. What did you do in Southampton?

MARIE
I used to sell flowers.

BUFORD
Flowers?

MARIE
Yes, it was a trick. I had to, because Mr. Rochester had sold me to ... to ... a brothel... from which I ran away...

BUFORD
A brothel?

MARIE
He said he needed money, because my father had been involved in a deal that went bad...

BUFORD is visibly uncomfortable now. He wants to get up, but his body is too weak.

BUFORD
Marie, could you help me, please. I need to get up.

MARIE
What for?

BUFORD
I just need to.

CONTINUED:

MARIE
(cold)
But I am not finished with my story yet.

BUFORD
I am listening.

MARIE
So I was sold to a brothel, a stinking brothel near the port. Every day drunken sailors, foreigners, and once in a while business people, or judges, and...

MARIE pauses and looks at BUFORD, who stares at her.

BUFORD
And...?

MARIE
Priests.

BUFORD
Not all are honorable, Marie.

MARIE
Oh, the one who came to me was!

FLASH BACK:

SOUTHAMPTON:

INT. RESTAURANT -- NIGHT (<u>REPEAT SAME SCENE FROM BEGINNING</u>)

Thick smoke waves through the room. The tables are filled with MEN, drinking, gambling, talking. In a corner he sees some well-dressed GENTLEMEN with young WHORES on their knees. JONATHAN orders a soup, bread, and water. While he eats silently, he observes his surroundings. A "FLOWER GIRL" (16), slender, pretty, with a bucket of flowers comes to his table. She looks at him, scanning his face to see whether he understands this kind of soliciting business.

FLOWER GIRL
Please, would you like to buy some, sir? My rose is fresh.

JONATHAN, (not getting this soliciting act by a prostitute), buys a rose.

(CONTINUED)

CONTINUED:

Suddenly the FLOWER GIRL begins to sob (to keep his attention). Jonathan tries to calm her. An OLDER WOMAN (part of the act) comes by and takes the girl by her hand.

OLDER WOMAN
Sorry, Father. But her mother died a week ago. The girl is still up-set. Sorry. Let's go, girl. Be quiet.

JONATHAN swirls the rose in his hand until the head breaks off. He is up-set. He eats his meal.

BACK TO:

INT. SEEDY HOTEL ROOM -- PANAMA CITY -- DAY

MARIE is looking serious.

MARIE
But it was all a trick, you know.

FLASH BACK:

SOUTHAMPTON:

INT. RESTAURANT -- NIGHT (<u>REPEAT SCENE</u>)

JONATHAN pays for his meal and steps outside the restaurant.

EXT. SOUTHAMPTON -- STREET (<u>REPEAT SCENE</u>)

Across the street, the OLDER WOMAN whispers something into the ears of the "FLOWER GIRL" who nods and walks swiftly after Jonathan. She catches up with him, passes by and then runs into him, trips and falls in front of Jonathan. He almost stumbles over her. The "Flower Girl" starts sobbing. Jonathan recognizes her and he bends down.

BACK TO:

INT. SEEDY HOTEL ROOM -- PANAMA CITY -- DAY

MARIE is looking intently at BUFORD, to see what his reaction might be.

MARIE
The priest took me to his hotel, and first I thought, that he wanted me...
(MORE)

(CONTINUED)

CONTINUED:

MARIE (cont'd)
but then he was a gentleman, a real gentleman, someone who just wanted to take care of me...

FLASH BACK:

SOUTHAMPTON:

EXT. SOUTHAMPTON STREET -- NIGHT (REPEAT SAME SCENE)

FLOWER GIRL
(grabbing his hand)
Where could I go now? I am all alone. Please help me, Father!

JONATHAN
(firm)
Come.

He grabs the GIRL by the hand, and they walk off. Keeping a distance, BUFORD is following them.

JONATHAN (cont'd)
You can stay with me tonight. I have a room. But I'll leave tomorrow. I am Father Jonathan White. And what's your name?

FLOWER GIRL
They call me Dolly. . . Nice to meet you, Father.

BACK TO:

INT. SEEDY HOTEL ROOM -- PANAMA CITY -- DAY

MARIE
I told him they call me Dolly.

MARIE laughs out loud. She looks a BUFORD who lies in his bed in dead silence.

MARIE
He was so sweet, so gentle. So sweet and gentle...

FLASH BACK:

SOUTHAMPTON:

INT. HOTEL ROOM -- NIGHT (REPEAT SAME SCENE)

Both enter the room.

JONATHAN
(firm)
Now, you clean yourself up and then you sleep over there on that bed.

He points to a second bed in the corner.

FLOWER GIRL
Yes, Father.

JONATHAN
What's your real name, little girl?

FLOWER GIRL
Marie, Father.

JONATHAN
You seem to have a French accent...

But before he gets an answer, the GIRL disappears in the bathroom. Meanwhile, JONATHAN kneels in front of his bed, praying silently. When the GIRL reappears, washed, her hair flowing, her dress a bit different, Jonathan is still praying with his eyes closed. The girl walks to the bed and lies down. She pulls the blanket over her body. Jonathan finishes his prayer, opens his eyes and gets up. He looks at the girl. Then he goes into the bathroom and closes the door. While he is in the bathroom, the girl takes off her clothes, but then she pulls the blanket up to her chin again. When Jonathan returns, he looks at the girl again, who has by now closed her eyes, then he lies down in the other bed and blows out the candle. Then he undresses himself, puts the cross on the night stand, slips under the sheet, folds his hands, and closes his eyes. He drifts into sleep.

BACK TO:

INT. SEEDY HOTEL ROOM -- PANAMA CITY -- DAY

MARIE looks at BUFORD. He stares at the ceiling.

MARIE
And the next morning the priest left, he even put some money for me on the table.

(CONTINUED)

CONTINUED:

BUFORD
(clearing his throat)
His name was ... Jonathan White, wasn't it.

MARIE
And after he had left, there was a commotion at the door, followed by an argument, and suddenly the door was thrown open, and a man walked in...

FLASH BACK TO:

SOUTHAMPTON:

INT. HOTEL ROOM -- MORNING

MARIE (O.S.)
And he tore away the blanket, and he saw that I was naked...

BUFORD is pulling a knife from his boot and presses it against MARIE'S throat. And then he rapes her...

BACK TO:

INT. SEEDY HOTEL ROOM -- PANAMA CITY -- DAY

MARIE stares at BUFORD.

MARIE
And when it was all over, he took the knife and cut my cheek... Right here, do you see it...?

She bends over to BUFORD to show him the scar. Buford looks away.

MARIE
... Of course you know where the scar is...

MARIE gets up and walks to the kitchen table. She picks up the bread knife and walks back to BUFORD'S bed.

MARIE (cont'd)
He did it like that...

(CONTINUED)

CONTINUED:

With a quick slash, SHE cuts BUFORD'S cheek. Buford cries. Blood is flowing from the wound.

MARIE (cont'd)
And when he walked out, he even took the money the priest had left me...

BUFORD has begun to sob.

MARIE (cont'd)
A bit later the priest came into the room.

FLASH BACK:

SOUTHAMPTON:

INT. HOTEL ROOM -- MORNING

MARIE (O.S.)
He was all beaten up. In his hands, he was holding a shirt, a jacket and trousers... Guess who's? I took care of him, washed his bruises and bandaged them.

MARIE is helping JONATHAN WHITE. With great tenderness, she washes his bruises and cleans him up.

BACK TO:

INT. SEEDY HOTEL ROOM -- PANAMA CITY -- DAY

MARIE
(cold as ice)
And then, we sat down and plotted revenge!

FLASH BACK:

SOUTHAMPTON:

INT. HOTEL ROOM -- SOUTHAMPTON -- MORNING

MARIE and JONATHAN are sitting on the floor. Both are crying, comforting each other.

(CONTINUED)

CONTINUED:

MARIE
This is not just.

JONATHAN nods.

JONATHAN
You are right. This is evil, but the Lord will do us right. I am sure.

He hugs MARIE, and then tends to her wounded cheek.

JONATHAN
I am sure, the Lord will do us justice. I am very sure.

He looks past MARIE into the distance, but we see on her face that revenge is on her mind.

BACK TO:

INT. SEEDY HOTEL ROOM -- PANAMA CITY -- EVENING

A few hours have passed. It is evening now. BUFORD who has been smoking the laced opium all afternoon, is passed out. MARIE is looking at Buford who is lying silently and motionlessly in his bed. His eyes are closed, he breathes shallowly.

Marie walks to the kitchen and fetches a metal saw from underneath the sink. She disinfects it with pure alcohol, then she gets towels and a large oil lamp. She walks back to Buford's bed, throws back the blanket, pulls down his trousers and takes them off. She neatly folds the trousers and puts them into a corner on the floor. Then she disinfects his legs with the alcohol. She then grabs the metal saw...hesitates, and her hand sinks down. She starts crying...

DISSOLVE TO:

LATER

MARIE is sitting on the chair, watching BUFORD who is moaning and finally waking up.

MARIE
How do you like the opium I brought you?

(CONTINUED)

CONTINUED:

BUFORD
(confused)
I feel pain in my legs...

MARIE
Sorry, I thought it was stronger...
Here, take this.

He sighs and his head is tilting to the side. MARIE gives him the pipe, and BUFORD inhales several times deeply. After a while:

BUFORD
That's better. Still, I feel pain in my legs.

MARIE
You'll get used to it.

BUFORD
What did you say? I can't hear you very well. My head is humming, and I feel this pain in my legs.

MARIE
Can you see me?

BUFORD
My legs, I can't feel my legs...
pain, I feel pain...

MARIE
Can you still see?

BUFORD is opening his eyes wide.

BUFORD
I can still see. But what happened to my legs? I can't feel my legs, Marie! There is something burning down there...

MARIE
(ice-cold)
Then watch this!

MARIE gets up and walks to the adjacent door.

MARIE
Are you ready?

BUFORD
Ready for what?

(CONTINUED)

CONTINUED:

MARIE
You'll see...

She opens the door...

DISSOLVE TO:

EXT. LANDSCAPE (HIERONYMUS BOSCH-LIKE) -- DAY

A landscape of fire and burning, destruction, falling walls, exploding houses, people running for shelter, a tsunami of debris sweeping the landscape... BUFORD, dressed in a long white robe, is standing on an open field, hands outstretched, it is raining, first water, then the drops turn into blood. His robe is stained with blood, he tries to walk, but his feet don't move. Slowly, he is sinking into mud...

Then, suddenly, beautiful ANGELS are dancing, hand in hand, their dresses are floating in the wind, they smile and embrace each other, but after a while, the Angels turn into ZOMBIES. Some are now floating through the air on broomsticks, others are dancing to a DEVILISH MUSIC. Suddenly one ANGEL steps away from the group, runs down to a shoreline, kneels down and digs up mud and stones and throws them into the air, first moaning, then crying and lastly shrieking up to a mad crescendo...until the face of BUFORD is dug up and visible.

BUFORD (O.S.)
Marie, what is going on? What's happening to me? My legs are burning.

BUFORD moans and groans.

BUFORD'S FACE rises from the mud and turns into the sun, which is rising above mountains (MUSIC: Strauss, Also Sprach Zarathustra) and into the music steps through the door the REAL JONATHAN WHITE. He is dressed in red, like the DEVIL, with hooves and all, and he carries a SAW from which blood is dripping. He takes BUFORD and leads him to the Railroad Complex where he has to join the workers.

FLASH BACK:

EXT. RAILROAD COMPLEX -- COLON -- DAY

BUFORD is now standing up to his hip in the SWAMP. Mosquitoes are buzzing about, the noise from the near-by jungle (birds screeching, monkeys howling, etc.) is deafening.

(CONTINUED)

CONTINUED:

An ALLIGATOR is moving slowly towards Buford, who is terrified and screams...the alligator moves away, and in its mouth dangles a leg.

In the next vision, BUFORD is surrounded by a dozen CHINESE WORKERS who all smoke opium and give him the pipe, too. But the Chinese look scary and they stare at Buford, and when he smokes, they all begin to laugh eerily.

FLASH BACK:

INT. YANKEE TRAIL -- HOTEL ROOM -- NIGHT

BUFORD sees himself in the hotel room with LADY LENNOX. He is on his knees with a belt wrapped around his neck. Buford is naked and on his back are red marks from the whip. Lady Lennox is dressed in a fur coat, underneath she is naked also.

BUFORD
Please, no more beating, I beg you, please!

LADY LENNOX
You son of a bitch. I'll teach you!

She lashes out again and again, until his back is covered in blood.

FLASH BACK:

EXT. JUNGLE -- DAY

BUFORD is surrounded by INDIANS who cut open his belly and tear out his guts which are nailed to a tree. Then he is whipped around it. Slowly, the guts are wrapping around the tree, until Buford collapses.

FLASH BACK:

INT. BARRACK -- DAY

In the next vision, BUFORD is in DR. RUBBER'S barrack where the sick lie. He is one of them, looking greenish, throwing up, his body covered with excrement. The MEN moan and cry in pain and despair. DR. RUBBER walks in with an ASSISTANT, both are dressed in Buford coats. They take Buford with them to the barrack where the corpses are "pickled". Buford is put into a bathtub and the solution is poured over him. He is finally covered, except his face.

(CONTINUED)

CONTINUED:

Both Dr. Rubber and his assistant then take Buford out of the bathtub and lay him on a bed. The assistant now holds a knife in his hand and begins to flay Buford, until there is only a SKELETON left.

BUFORD (O.S.)
(screaming)
Marie, help, what is happening? My legs? I can't move my legs! Where is all this blood coming from?

BACK TO:

INT. SEEDY HOTEL ROOM -- PANAMA CITY -- NIGHT

BUFORD opens his eyes, JONATHAN WHITE, dressed in priest garb, is sitting next to him on the bed.

JONATHAN WHITE
Well, well...at last we meet... again.

BUFORD
(horrified)
What are you doing to me?

JONATHAN WHITE
Do you remember a certain morning in Southampton, about a year ago?

BUFORD
(gasping, horrified)
Listen, I was drunk and in a rage...

JONATHAN WHITE
So, drunk and in a rage. And that gives you license to beat me up and rape a young girl...? And cut her face...?
(beat)
By the way, what is your name..?

BUFORD
Buford, Robert Buford. Listen...

JONATHAN WHITE
(interrupting)
Robert Buford... Well, Robert Buford. It is time for us to leave.

JONATHAN looks at MARIE, who nods in agreement.

(CONTINUED)

CONTINUED:

JONATHAN WHITE (cont'd)
I am a priest, a man of God, and of course, I have forgiven you some time ago. By the way, Marie and I are going to San Francisco, I hear it is nice there.

BUFORD is looking to JONATHAN, then to MARIE in bewilderment. Slowly, his hands are moving down the blanket toward his legs. Buford's face expresses horror. His hands reach down to his legs, he bends up and reaches further down... He looks at MARIE, who stares back.

MARIE
He might have forgiven you...(beat) But I haven't!

She walks to the bed and tears away the blanket. Both of BUFORD'S legs are cut off below the knees. Bloody towels are wrapped around the stumps. Buford looks at his legs, then, sinking back into the pillows, emits an other-worldly scream...then he passes out.

DISSOLVE TO:

INT. OPIUM DEN

... BUFORD sits upright on his bed, and both his hands grab his legs. He throws off the blanket and he stares at them. He feels them, as if they weren't there, (but of course, they are...), then he sighs and sinks back onto the bed.

He starts sobbing...then he looks at the table with the opium pipe and the empty bottle of absinthe. His sobbing stops and a few moments later he begins to laugh, then he begins to cry again. His emotion changes between crying and laughter.

Out of a dark corner, the GREEN FAIRY is floating to his bed. She sits down and looks at Buford, then she gives him a kiss on the forehead and floats away...

GREEN FAIRY
(whispering)
Bye, bye my dreamer...

FADE OUT:

THE END

23938644R00055

Made in the USA
Middletown, DE
09 September 2015